MW00561701

I CHOOSE
to Calm My Anger

DEDICATED TO B.L.

I CHOOSE SERIES

ELIZABETH ESTRADA

I was angry at my mom and **dad**,
My parents said, "No," which made me **mad**.
I asked to play games with Aiden my best **friend**,
But chores after school were the rules, and wouldn't **bend**.

I begged, but no reason I could **find**
Could change my parents' **mind**.
I walked to school, a frown on my **face**,
I kicked a can and sent it to **space**.

I opened the door and some friends said, "**Hello**
I just ignored them and kept walking real **slow**.
I threw my backpack onto my **desk**.
It looked like this day would be quite a **test**.

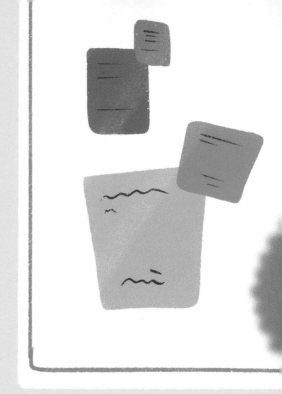

I went to my class, sat in the back of the **room**.
I just couldn't concentrate, I was so full of **gloom**.
A new boy sat near me and said, "Hi, I'm **Ray**.
I snapped at him and said, "Not **today**!"

At recess my friend, Liam, asked me, "What's **wrong**?
"Life's not always easy, but we have to be **strong**."
I can't help it, I can feel the anger boiling inside **me**.
"It's okay to feel anger, keeping it inside can make you **unhappy**."

"Accepting anger is important if we want to control **it**.
Just take three deep breaths and you won't want to **hit**.
Then, count up to ten, and you'll show anger the **door**.
Think of a happy place, and you'll be calm once **more**."

So I thanked my friend for his **help**.
I decided to be stronger than anger **itself**.
I breathed in and out deeply, then counted to **ten**,
And thought of a happy place to find my **zen**.

This helped me feel calmer and my anger had **eased**,
I walked to the playground where I sometimes got **teased**.
This was part of the problem that made me get **cross**,
I was bullied by a kid whose nickname was "**Boss**."

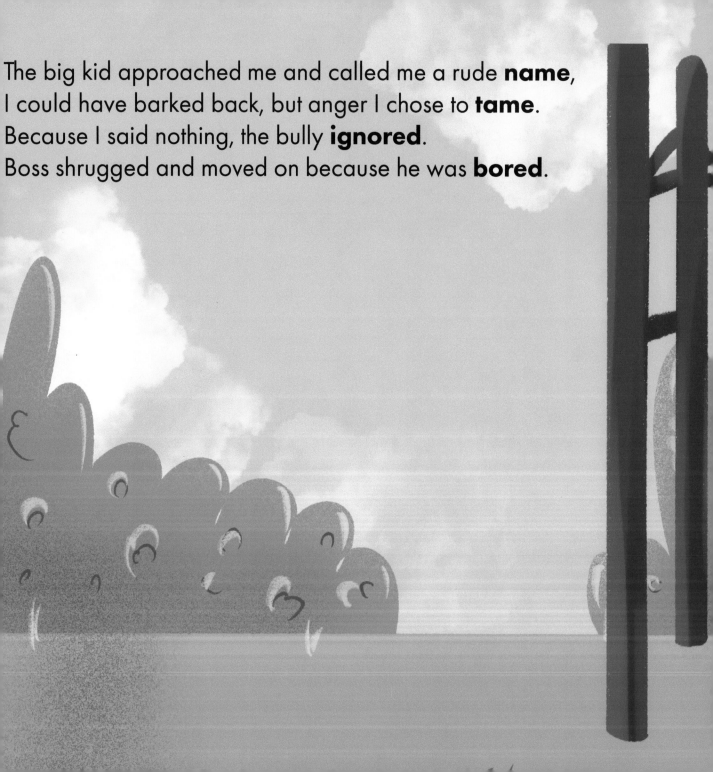

The big kid approached me and called me a rude **name**,
I could have barked back, but anger I chose to **tame**.
Because I said nothing, the bully **ignored**.
Boss shrugged and moved on because he was **bored**.

I felt surprised that this approach **worked**,
I had defeated my anger and my spirits **perked**.
Then, when I found out I didn't get picked for the **team**.
My hands sweat, and my anger grew **steam**.

But then I remembered to breathe in and **out**.
After I counted to ten, I no longer wanted to **shout**.
I knew what to do when I couldn't get my **way**,
I can keep my cool, come what **may**.

I never knew I could control my **anger**.
Thanks to my friend for helping me become **stronger**.
I learned it's okay to be angry and upset, **too**.
But it's up to me on how I respond and what I **do**.

I am calm.

I can breathe.

CALM

When I am mindful, I am aware of my feelings. When I am aware, I can accept and then manage my emotions.

I can visualize.

HIGH FIVE BREATH

This tool helps you stay calm by slowly breathing in and out.

For adults and children both...

1

Starting at the outside edge of your thumb, breathe in and use your index finger to trace up to the top. When you breathe out, slowly trace down the other side.

2

Keep breathing in and out, tracing up and down for a total of five breaths.

Keep going up and down until you reach the other side of your hand.

Begin here, at the outer edge of your thumb.

Dear Reader,

Thank you for reading my book. I hope you enjoyed a "I Choose to Calm My Anger." I spent fifteen years piecing together resources and ideas to help young children cope with big emotions.

So please tell me what you liked and even what you disliked. What kind of emotion should be in my next book?

I love to receive messages from my readers. Please write to me at Elizabethestradainfo@gmail.com

I would also greatly appreciate it if you could review my book.
Your feedback matters a lot to me!

With love,
Elizabeth

CPSIA information can be obtained
at www.ICGtesting.com
Printed in the USA

A FRIENDSHIP STORY

HEART & MIND

Written by Nishi Singhal

Creator of the Heart & Mind Series

Illustrated by Lera Munoz

PRECOCITY PRESS

Sign up here for a free Joy Journal for kids!
To help them further create a partnership between their
hearts and minds. www.joyparade.co/freebie

Editor: Lorraine Wadman
Creative Director and Designer: Susan Shankin
Illustrator: Lera Munoz

ISBN: 978-1-7373539-7-3

Library of Congress Control Number: 2020911581

Published by Precocity Press
Venice, CA 90291

First edition. Printed and bound in the United States of America

Heart and Mind are the very best of friends
and have been all their lives.

They each have their own special qualities
and keep each other balanced.

Mind is great at learning and solving problems.

Mind knows that if you tie your shoelaces,
you will not trip and fall on them.

Mind is also great at taking action.

If Mind wanted to make banana bread,
it would start by taking out the ingredients.

HEART TALKS TO US THROUGH JOY & LOVE

Heart is amazing at loving you.

It doesn't matter if you trip and fall on your shoelaces
or burn the banana bread,
Heart loves YOU exactly the way you are.

Heart is great at being in the HERE and NOW.

This means Heart doesn't worry
about yesterday or tomorrow.

When you follow your heart,
you feel joy in the HERE and NOW.

If Heart feels the spark to dance,
but Mind thinks that it will look silly
since it is not a REAL dancer...

Heart can tell Mind that it will love
without any judgment.

Mind is always ready to take action if Heart
is having a hard time knowing what it wants.

Mind will hold Heart's hand and take one step in
any direction until they know what Heart wants.

When Heart and Mind work together,
life feels fun and easier.

One day, Heart and Mind decided
to spend the day apart.

Heart wanted to lie in the grass
and watch the clouds passing by.

Mind thought this was too boring and
decided to find something else to do.

Mind kept thinking and thinking

and walking and walking.

Mind thought about
going swimming, then Mind
thought about how it wasn't a great swimmer,
then Mind thought about how it should really
take swimming lessons, then Mind thought about
whether to take swimming lessons at the pool or
at the lake, then Mind thought about . . .

Mind kept thinking until the sun started to set.

"Oh no, it's time for me to go home.
But I didn't get to do anything fun!"

"Hi, Mind!"

"Oh, hi Heart"

"It looks like you had a lovely walk today!"

"What do you mean?"

"I was on top of that big hill, and I
could see you walking around the grassy field.
It looked like a lot of fun!"

"I wasn't able to enjoy it.
I was too busy thinking about
what I should be doing with my day."

Heart smiled.

"Remember what I always say:
Enjoy where you are right now. Because right now is your
greatest gift. That's why we call it The Present."

"Did you enjoy watching the clouds pass by?"

"I did! But soon after you left,
I felt like going for a swim. So I went to the lake.
When I got there, Ms. Lifeguard was
teaching a swimming class, so I joined.
After the class, I decided to watch the sunset!"

"Whoa. You did a lot today. You had a busy day."

"I had a FUN day because I followed my joy.
But I felt like you were with me every step of the way."

"When I felt the spark of what to do next.
I asked myself: What would Mind do?
since you are amazing at taking action."

16

"That's why we are best friends.
I help you focus on what you enjoy in the present,
and you help me take action."

ideas

Learning

inspiration

action

creating

JOY LOVE JOY

Mind thought about it for a second
and suddenly saw the night sky above.

"Hey, wouldn't it be fun to lie in the grass
and look for shooting stars?"

Heart and Mind lay in the grass watching the stars.
And whenever Mind started to think too much, Heart
reminded Mind of the joy of being in the present.

That's what friends are for.

DISCUSSION QUESTIONS

☆ What have you learned through your mind? How to tell time? How to measure ingredients for baking a cake? The names of your classmates?

☆ What types of action does your mind like to take? Does it like to write? Swim? Run? Play the piano?

☆ How does your heart show you love? The next time your mind judges you for making a mistake, like misspelling a word, allow your heart to love you.

☆ What does it mean to be in the HERE and NOW? Are you planning what to do after dinner? Are you thinking about what your friend said to you at school?

☆ How does it feel when you are in the HERE and NOW? Do you feel more joy and love? Peaceful and calm?

☆ Has your mind ever kept thinking and thinking, and you wished you could turn it off? What did you do to turn it off?

☆ Do you think Heart and Mind are good partners? Why?

EXERCISES

KEEPING HEART & MIND BALANCED

Practice listening to your heart and use your mind to take action.

- ☆ Close your eyes.
- ☆ Take some deep breaths.
- ☆ Let thoughts and mental pictures pass by.
- ☆ Allow yourself to relax.
- ☆ Ask your heart, "What do you want to do right now?
- ☆ Wait and listen for a response.
- ☆ Use your mind to take action.

Ideas from your heart can come through as words, images, feelings, or a joyful burst of action!

LIVE IN THE HERE & NOW

Practice living in the present. Start with exercise above. If your mind wanders into thinking about yesterday and tomorrow, come back into the present.

- ☆ Be a lion! Take a deep breath in through your nose, open your mouth, and roar the air out.
- ☆ Place one hand on your heart and the other hand on your belly, close your eyes, and stare into the blackness.
- ☆ Pick a color! Look around and find everything you can that is that color.
- ☆ Pet your dog or cuddle a favorite stuffed animal!

Hello, Caregivers!

Thank you for choosing to share this book with your little ones and yourself! The more present we can become, the more we increase our capacity for joy.

I wrote this book for young people to understand that they are not their minds. They have a mind that can perform a variety of tasks but ultimately, they exist beyond it. When the mind can be viewed as a tool available to us, we can then view moments of anxious thinking as the overuse of this one tool.

Along with overthinking, over-doing becomes a deterrent from being present in the moment. Believing that we are not complete without checking off the endless to-do list becomes conditioned within us if we do not accept that we are unconditionally loved right now. This book helps to teach young ones that regardless of what they do or do not do, they are complete, whole, and loved right now.

I hope you and your loved ones have enjoyed this first book in my Heart & Mind series! These books are meant to remind us how to live joyfully through the tools we already have inside us.

Love,
Nishi

ABOUT THE AUTHOR

NISHI SINGHAL has a bachelor's degree in psychology from the University of Michigan and a master's degree in public health from the University of Illinois at Chicago. Nishi is a public health expert, an integrated consciousness coach, and certified yoga teacher. Nishi has studied psychology, consciousness, and neuroscience with Joe Dispenza, Eckhart Tolle, and Deepak Chopra. She has worked with various nonprofits on bettering communities and currently serves as The Lively Community Foundation's director.

Inspired by her work with children through teaching yoga, Nishi created Joy Parade, an online space dedicated to teaching children and their caretakers how to bring presence into their day-to-day living. Nishi wrote *A Friendship Story: Heart & Mind* to introduce the concept of presence so that anyone (big or small) can live a more balanced and joyful life. Nishi's mission is to create light and fun ways for young people to view life through writing and one-on-one coaching.

Visit **JoyParade.co** to learn more and for additional resources.

ABOUT THE ILLUSTRATOR

LERA MUNOZ is an illustrator specializing in children's illustration. She loves to create playful characters and imaginary worlds that inspire young minds. Her work is perfect for storytelling and has been described as charming and full of warmth.

Lera lives in France with her husband and 4-year-old daughter. Being from Russia and now living in France, Lera takes the best from both cultures. In her free time, she likes to read, meditate, and travel. Her life is filled with domestic warmth and smiles of family and friends. For more information, visit leramunoz.com.

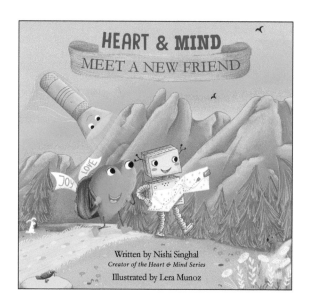

HEART & MIND: MEET A NEW FRIEND

The two friends are back! This time Heart & Mind meet a new friend, Awareness, a superhero flashlight who teaches them how to release heavy emotions like anger, sadness, and fear. Read along as your child develops new skills of letting their emotions pass like clouds in the sky so that they can live a more joyous life!

TESTIMONIALS

Heart, mind, and awareness are critical for the wellness and success of everyone's life, children and adults alike. This beautiful book brings insightful awareness to this important topic.

~DR. RULIN XIU, Quantum Physicist, founder of Tao Science and Authorr

This book is a great way to teach kids the power of managing their emotions and how different parts of them can work together to do so. It is very well written and the illustrations are darling!

~ANALISA JAYASEKERA, Licensed Marriage and Family Therapist

Children all over the world will be overjoyed to meet their new friend. As they grow, getting to know their own characters and embracing more of themselves through story, their new friend(s) will go very far in helping them to feel comforted, reassured, and able to interpret the many thoughts and emotions they have to deal with each and every day. Brilliantly illustrated, friendly, and emotionally moving, you will enjoy sharing with your kiddos about their friends and how to live a balanced life with presence and focus.

~KELLY PIERCE, Certified Life & Business Coach, Reiki Master, and RTT Practitioner

I CHOOSE
to Calm My Anger

I
CHOOSE
SERIES

ELIZABETH

CPSIA information can be obtained
at www.ICGtesting.com
Printed in the USA
BVHW021954190821
614611BV00035B/1228